The Poet Upstairs

By Judith Ortiz Cofer

Illustrations by Oscar Ortiz

Piñata Books
Arte Público Press
Houston, Texas

Publication of *The Poet Upstairs* is funded by a grant from the City of Houston through the Houston Arts Alliance. We are grateful for their support.

Piñata Books are full of surprises!

Piñata Books
An Imprint of Arte Público Press
University of Houston
4902 Gulf Fwy, Bldg 19, Rm 100
Houston, Texas 77204-2004

Cover design by Mora Des!gn

Cofer, Judith Ortiz, 1952-
   The Poet Upstairs / by Judith Ortiz Cofer; illustrations by Oscar Ortiz.
      p.   cm.
   Summary: When a poet moves into the apartment above hers, young Juliana asks to meet her and together they write poems of tropical birds and a river that flows to the sea, typing out words that change the world, if only for a while.
   ISBN 978-1-55885-704-9 (alk. paper)
   [1. Poetry—Fiction. 2. Authorship—Fiction. 3. Imagination—Fiction.] I. Ortiz, Oscar, (José Oscar Ortiz), 1964- ill. II. Title.
   PZ7.O765Poe 2012
   [E]—dc23
                                                                                    2012012709
                                                                                    CIP

Printed in China in May 2012–July 2012 by Creative Printing USA Inc.
12 11 10 9 8 7 6 5 4 3 2 1

> "y mi niñez fue toda un poema en el río,
> y un río en el poema de mis primeros sueños."
>
> —*El Río Grande de Loiza*, **Julia De Burgos**

This book is for my grandson, Elias John, and with love and gratitude to his parents, Tanya and Dory, who read to Eli every day.

As always, I want to thank John Cofer for his constant encouragement of my work.

Mil gracias to my *compañeras* Billie Bennett Franchini, Kathryn Locey and Erin Christian who offered their comments and expertise as this book evolved over time, until it came to fruition.

—JOC

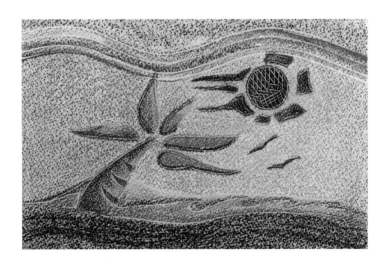

To my dear wife Wina and my beautiful children Oscar-Giovanni and Nitshell. Your unconditional love and patience keeps my universe together. *Los amo.*

—OO

One day, a poet moved into the apartment upstairs in the building where a little girl lived with her mother. The girl, Juliana, was too sick to go to her first day of school. Her bed faced the window so she could see the street.

"Who's the lady with all the books, Mami?" she asked her mother, who was getting ready to go to work. Her mother was a nurse for the old people in their building.

"I heard that she's a famous poet, that she lived on an island, like me," Mami answered.

They watched the poet, a tall lady in a red coat and red hat, carry boxes of books and papers from a car. They heard her going up and down the stairs.

"A writer?" Juliana was excited when she heard this. She loved books, and her mother read to her in both Spanish and English.

"I heard that she's writing a book, *hija*. We must not bother her." But seeing her daughter's look of disappointment, she added, "Maybe we'll meet her. But first, you have to get better."

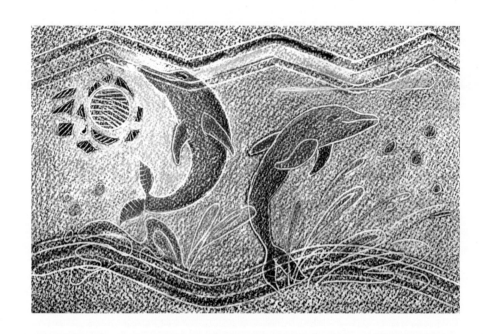

After her mother went to work, Juliana heard the sound of a typewriter clicking and clacking and the poet walking around upstairs. She listened until she fell asleep.

Juliana had a dream.

She dreamed that her bed was floating on a river, a wide river that took her through a grove of palm trees and down a field where cows grazed on green grass. A big, warm sun shone on Juliana's face.

The currents of air made her feel like she could fly. And in her dream, Juliana did fly. The bed became a kite. Its long tail was her multicolored blanket. She guided her flying bed over a mountain range that divided a beautiful island down the middle, like a brown belt. She drifted over an ocean of turquoise blue water, where dolphins leaped into the air and danced as she flew above.

When her mother came in to feel her head for fever, Juliana told her of the dream. Her mother said, "That's a beautiful dream, *hija*. You dreamed of my island. I think a happy dream means you will soon be well. I'm going back to work now, but will return to check on you during my break. Call me if you need me."

Juliana was alone again. It started to snow. From her bed, she saw people bundled up and walking with their heads down. The cars glided slowly on the slippery streets. There was nothing exciting to see except the mounds of gray slush. The whole world seemed frozen, and Juliana started to feel lonely.

She heard the sound of a chair scraping the floor and then the music of the typewriter keys. Juliana closed her eyes and imagined that each letter the poet typed was a brushstroke, painting a picture in her head.

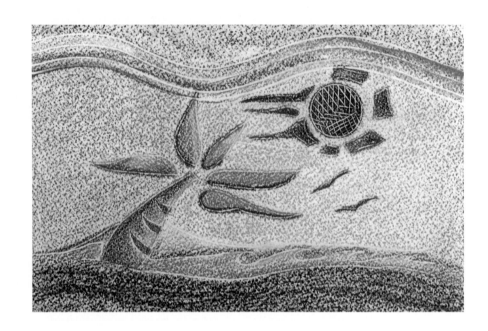

Listening to the sounds of the typewriter, Juliana heard a song inside her head. It was a song in Spanish, a song of a tiny tropical island sitting on the ocean like a green button on a blue dress.

It was a song of the red hibiscus flower opening slowly, like a mouth about to sing, then curling up tight like a baby sleeping at the end of the day.

It was a song of warm afternoon rain showers that washed the world and made everything look brand new, and of beaches of white sands, and of waters the same blue as the sky, like the ones she had seen in a book about the island where her mother was born.

Juliana felt better, and when her mother returned from work, she asked for paper and coloring pencils. Juliana did not know how to write all the words, but as she listened to the poet work, she drew pictures of what she was seeing in her mind.

Juliana drew a big shade tree with bright orange flowers, like a big umbrella.

Juliana drew a lake, where all the fish shone like stars in a clear night sky.

She drew a tiny green frog, no bigger than her thumb, sitting on a palm frond, singing after a rain shower.

She drew herself under the palm tree, reading a book called *Poemas*.

When Juliana was feeling well enough to get out of bed, she took the drawings upstairs and slid them under the poet's door.

The next day, a piece of paper came in under the little girl's door. It was a drawing of a lady wearing a red hat with papers in her hand. And there was another, smaller, figure and an arrow pointing up a flight of stairs. It was an invitation from the poet to visit her!

Juliana asked Mami if it was okay to visit the poet, and her mother said, "Yes, *hija*. I have met the poet upstairs. I told her that you love books."

"*Gracias*, Mami."

The girl ran up the stairs and knocked on the poet's door. The poet opened it. She was wearing a large red sweater and a red cap over her black hair. Her fingers stuck out of blue gloves, whose tips had been cut off so she could type. It was very cold in her apartment. The heater under the window was not making any noise, and the windows had frost on them.

Juliana saw the small table in the middle of the room with a black typewriter on it. A bare light bulb shone above it. There were stacks of books all around the tiny apartment.

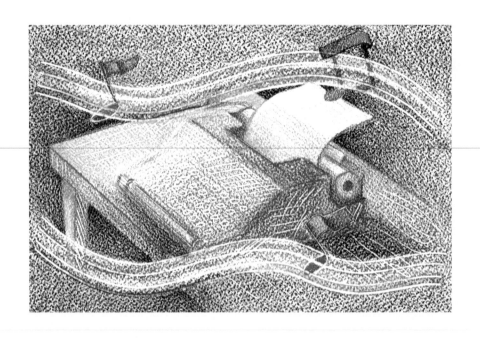

"I love your poems," Juliana said to the poet.

"You have read my poems?" the poet asked.

"No, I have not. I have seen your poems in my head, and I have dreamed about the pictures you make with words."

"Yes, that happens with poetry sometimes. Poems can get into your head like songs."

"What do you mean?"

The poet took Juliana's hand and led her to the work table. "I'll show you how I write poems. Sit here next to me." The poet pulled another chair next to her writing desk. They sat down in front of the typewriter.

"What would you like to write about?" she asked Juliana.

"I like birds."

From her window, Juliana saw only the pigeons that roosted on the rooftops and sat on wires, but she had seen pictures of tropical birds with feathers in all the colors of the rainbow in her mother's books about her island. These were the birds she wanted to see when she closed her eyes.

The poet wrote:

In an island garden
picaflores dart around in circles,
like flying jewels. Emeralds, rubies,
sapphires and diamonds twinkling in the sunlight.
They hang by their beaks in a circle,
sipping nectar from the flowers,
like a necklace on a queen.

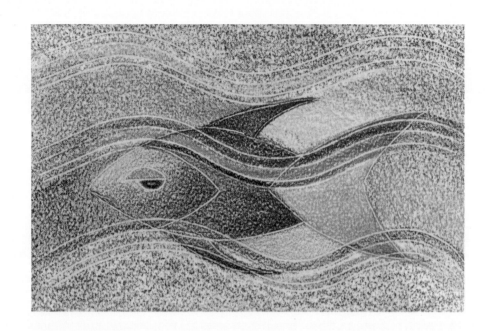

As Juliana watched the poet's fingers touching each letter, and the letters making words, she imagined tiny sparks of colorful lights flashing off the keys.

"Think of a big yellow sun shining down on us," the poet said.

The room filled with light, and Juliana started to feel warm, as if the sun were shining right above them instead of just a single light bulb hanging from the ceiling.

"Can I try it?" Juliana asked.

"Yes. I'll help you find the right keys. What do you want to write about now?"

"About a big river."

"Yes. I like rivers. I know a big river. As a little girl, I would go to this river to watch the fish dancing under the water and to imagine I was a bird following the river to the sea."

The poet and the little girl worked together on a poem about a river that leads to the sea. As they made pictures with words, the walls of the tiny apartment melted, and outside a great river swelled and ran down the street. The girl felt the desk and the chairs start to float downstream.

The buildings became a mountain range, and the sidewalks turned into rich, black earth. As the girl and the poet worked on the poem, the words became whatever they imagined. Lampposts turned into palm trees. Seagulls, parrots and nightingales, all the birds the girl could name, circled around them. The poet wrote the names of flowers, and they sprouted from the rich black earth: orchids, roses, hibiscus and daisies. A big yellow sun grew brighter and warmer, until they had to take off their hats and gloves.

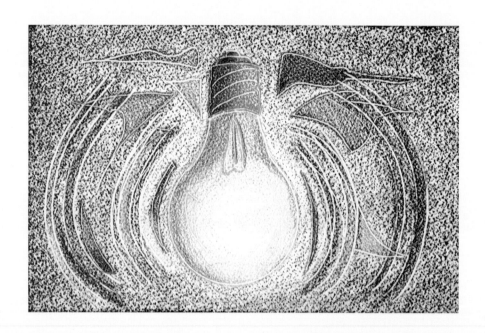

When they reached the ocean, and there was nothing but blue water as far as they could see, the poet said, "This poem is finished. It's time to go back."

As she pulled the paper out of the typewriter, the river dried into the concrete of the street; the mountains became the buildings of their neighborhood. As they stood up from their chairs, the walls surrounded them, and the sun dimmed into a light bulb again. It got colder as the city in winter returned outside the window. They put their gloves and hats back on, and they found themselves back at the desk in the poet's cold apartment.

The little girl shivered. She missed being in the poem.

The poet said, "Now you know how to write a poem. First, you have to believe that words can change the world."

"If other people read this poem, will they travel on the river to the sea, too?"

"The journey will be different for each reader. I will not be there to guide them as I did you. What they see may be different from what we saw. But it will still be a poem about a river that leads to the sea."

"Will you take my mother down the river?"

The poet lifted the pages of poetry from her desk and gave them to the girl.

"You can do it. You can take her and anyone else you choose back to the great river, and that river will always take you somewhere new."

That afternoon, Juliana showed the poem to her mother. Mami looked out of the window, as if she were seeing the world change outside, and said, "Yes, *hija*, I know this river. I played on the banks of El Gran Río when I was a child. I can still feel the warm mud on my toes. I used to pretend I was a mermaid swimming to the ocean."

"Mami, I have an idea. Let's go to El Gran Río together."

Then the girl asked her mother to help her write a poem, and as they put down each word, they felt the power of the river carrying them to every place they imagined. They played on the warm mud beside it and swam together in the river her mother remembered.

After she went back to school, Juliana did not see the poet again. She heard the typewriter late into the night, and the words she imagined became part of her dreams. But the poet did not invite her back to her apartment. Juliana knew that she was working on a book of poems and that she should not disturb her.

The girl worked on her own stories and poems as she listened to the poet upstairs. She remembered that words changed their world, even if only for a little time.

One day, Juliana did not hear the song of the typewriter. She did not hear the poet at all. Mami told her that the poet was no longer in the apartment upstairs. Juliana imagined her floating down her beloved river to another place she wanted to see.

After the poet left, Juliana never felt lonely again. The lesson the poet had taught her, that a poem is like a magic carpet that can take you anywhere in the world and let you be anything you want to be, was a gift that changed her life. When she was older, the girl would read the poet's books. She would find herself in one of the poems as *the little poet downstairs.* And one day, she would write a book of poems of her own, and she would dedicate it to the Poet Upstairs.

Photo courtesy of Isidor Ruderfer

Judith Ortiz Cofer, the Regents' and Franklin Professor of English and Creative Writing at the University of Georgia, is an award-winning poet, novelist and prose writer whose work deals with her bilingual, bicultural experience as a Puerto Rican woman living on the Mainland. She is the author of numerous books, including her first picture book, *¡A bailar!/Let's Dance!*; *Animal Jamboree: Latino Folktales/La fiesta de los animales: leyendas latinas*; *Silent Dancing: A Partial Remembrance of a Puerto Rican Childhood*, included in The New York Public Library's *Books for the Teen Age 1991* and recipient of a PEN citation, Martha Albrand Award for non-fiction and a Pushcart Prize; and *An Island Like You*, recipient of the Pura Belpré Award and named an ALA Best Book for Young Adults, a *School Library Journal* Best Book of the Year and an ALA Quick Picks for Reluctant Young Adult Readers. Other books for young adults include *The Year of Our Revolution, Call Me María* and *The Meaning of Consuelo*.

Oscar Ortiz was born in Manhattan, New York. He was raised and educated in Caguas, Puerto Rico. He is a graduate of the Art Instruction Schools in Minneapolis, MN. He currently resides in Indian Trail, North Carolina, with his wife and children. A dog and three cats have found their way into their home, too. When he's not painting, he's drawing or pondering on the next piece. His mind is in a constant creative green light mode. If you wish to snap him out of his artistic trance just mention the magic word . . . *café*! You can see more of his colorful work at www. oscarortiz.com.